THE PEAR TREE
THE BIRCH TREE
AND THE
BARBERRY BUSH

by Alois Carigiet

New York   Henry Z. Walck, Incorporated   1967

This book is about Domenic Tubak and his wife, and their two children, Victor and Babette.

It is the story, too, of Creak and Croak, the crows that nested in the pear tree, of Cutpurse and Pickpocket, the magpies that lived in the birch tree, and especially of Brownie and Whitethroat, the two hedge sparrows who built their nest in the prickly branches of the little barberry bush.

Alois Carigiet

In Canterdun, high up in the Grison Alps of Switzerland, there stood a little house. An old pear tree overshadowed it on one side, and on the other towered an enormous birch tree. Birds lived in both these trees: two crows, Creak and Croak, nested in the top of the pear tree, while Cutpurse and Pickpocket the magpies had made their home in the birch tree.

A little barberry bush grew beneath the birch tree. It bore golden blossoms in the spring and fire-red berries in the autumn. Beside the pear tree and the birch tree it seemed small and useless; its berries were much too sour to eat and its twigs were too sparse and prickly to be used for firewood. But was it really so useless?

Domenic Tubak and his wife Nessa lived with their two children in the little house between the trees. When the sun shone, they liked to sit on the bench beside the birch tree. One day Father was reading the newspaper and smoking his pipe, while Mother knitted some warm gloves for the winter. Babette was sewing a patch on Victor's coat sleeve. Her mother had taught her to sew, although she was still only a little girl, and had given her a special bag for her needle and scissors, spools of thread and thimble. The bag was flame-red and decorated with glass beads. Babette loved it dearly and took it everywhere with her.

Victor was watching the birds in the sky overhead. He saw Pink the chaffinch flying across to the pear tree and wondered if he was going to build his nest there.

The chaffinch did build his nest in the pear tree, patiently collecting feathers, fibers, stalks and hair in his beak. Victor hoped there would be some eggs in the nest, or even some baby birds. If only he could take just one look. The tree was too high for him to climb, so he borrowed his father's ladder.

He was delighted to see three little eggs lying cozily in the nest and he longed for the day when they would hatch.

One spring day Babette was sitting under the birch tree sewing. Above her the magpies lay hidden. They had seen the glass beads shining on her little red sewing bag.

Suddenly Babette heard Victor calling, "Father, Mother, Babette, come quickly. The crows are raiding the chaffinches' nest." Babette ran as fast as she could to the pear tree, leaving her sewing behind her on the bench, together with her needle and scissors, her spools of thread and her thimble—and her treasured red bag.

Father and Mother came running from the fields; Father waved his stick while Mother clapped her hands and Victor shouted, "Nest robbers!" at the top of his voice. But it was no use. Creak and Croak had found Pink's nest and broken the eggs. Then they flew back to their own nest in the pear tree.

The family stood for a while, grieving for the ruined nest and the poor chaffinches, and then they went back to work. Victor whispered to himself, "Dear Pink, we have lost our beautiful nest and now there will be no baby birds."

When Babette got back to the birch tree, she found her sewing hanging by a corner from the bench, and needle and scissors, spools of thread and thimble scattered on the ground. But the little red bag was gone.

"Oh, wherever is my dear little bag?" said Babette, and her eyes filled with tears. Victor came to see what was the matter. He looked up at the birch tree where the magpies were hiding. "Do you have Babette's little bag?" he asked them.

A mocking caw was the only answer. It sounded like
                    "Tra-tra-la, tra-tra-lay,
                    Not a word I'm going to say."

Summer and autumn were almost over, and the leaves began to fall from the trees and the days grew cold. Domenic Tubak decided it was time to collect firewood for the winter. One day he took his saw and his ax and cut down the old pear tree. The crows shrieked in fury, but no one cared that their home was gone and they had to fly away.

Victor and Babette helped their father sort the lumber—big logs for the living-room stove and smaller ones for the kitchen range. It was very hard work.

They put the logs in a basket to drag them to the woodshed. When they got tired, Babette and Victor sat down on the edge of the basket, each one remembering private sorrows. Victor thought about the ruined chaffinches' nest, and Babette couldn't forget her little red sewing bag. Meanwhile it was getting foggy, and snow began to fall.

At first the snow looked like frosting on a cake, but it soon lay thick and everything disappeared under a soft white cloak. It snowed day and night, and the drifts were almost as high as a man. The branch of the birch tree that held the magpies' nest groaned under the weight of the snow.

One evening Mother had just put on the light in the living-room when there was a crash from the birch tree. Everyone ran to the window and peered out, but it was too dark to see what had happened.

That night it stopped snowing, and when Victor and Babette went out in the morning, the sun was shining on an enchanted world. In the middle of the sparkling whiteness lay the broken branch with the magpies' nest. The children waded through the snow to it. Suddenly Babette called joyfully, "The little bag!" There it was, gleaming red through the dark twigs of the nest. The glass beads shone like stars. Babette was delighted to have her treasure once more.

Winter was hard in the mountains, but at last spring arrived, bringing a carpet of brightly colored flowers. Soon the many birds who had spent the winter in warmer lands came flying back—goldfinches, robins, wagtails, and also a pair of hedge sparrows, Brownie and Whitethroat. They were all looking for somewhere to nest, and very soon Brownie and Whitethroat were the only ones with no home. Then Brownie saw a tiny opening in the barberry bush. The hedge sparrows crept through and began to build their nest inside the prickly little shrub.

When it was finished Whitethroat laid four eggs in the new nest, while Brownie proudly sang his spring song. They were very careful whenever they flew in or out because they wanted to make sure no one was watching—no crows, no magpies, and no four-legged nest robbers.

Only Victor knew where the hedge sparrows' nest was, and he kept their secret safe. Sometimes he would part the twigs of the bush very gently and then he could see White-throat on her nest.

After three weeks the tiny hedge sparrows hatched. Their little beaks opened wide as they clamored for food. "Me, me, me," they cried. Victor heard them and was worried in case a nest robber heard them too, for he remembered what had happened to the chaffinches.

The danger during the day came from the crows and magpies, but at night it was the owls who went hunting.

One midnight, Mouser, the cat from the next farm, prowled by the bush and then stopped. Did he hear something? When he tried to crawl inside the bush, the briers tangled in his fur. Mouser freed himself crossly and slunk off.

The next visitor was Reynard the fox, the great robber, on his nightly hunt. He smelt something good and stuck his head into the bush. Then he yelped for his nose was full of thorns. Whining, he loped away, while the moon laughed at him. "There you are, you cunning robber—the little barberry bush is stronger than the big trees."

At last the night's dangers were over and the sun rose. The baby hedge sparrows left their nest for the first time, and sat in a row on the fence. Brownie and Whitethroat flew to and fro with food to fill the fledglings' crying mouths. Victor proudly showed his sister the hedge sparrow family.

Now everything was calm and peaceful; the meadows were full of sunshine, and bees and butterflies danced in the air.

The hedge sparrows stayed in Canterdun all summer, but when the first frost of autumn turned the birch leaves to gold, Brownie and Whitethroat got ready to leave with their fledglings for warmer lands.

Father, Mother and the children came in from the fields. The evening wind was blowing through the birch tree, and one bough of golden leaves danced against the sky.

Victor looked up and saw the flock of little birds flying south. The rest of the family looked up too, and heard the birds calling in their own tongue, "Good-by, dear children of Canterdun. We will come back in the spring, when the barberry bush is in bloom again."